D0269236

The Winter Adventure

Diane Redmond

RED FOX

A Red Fox Book

Published by Random House Children's Books
20 Vauxhall Bridge Road, London SW1V 2SA

A division of The Random House Group Ltd
London Melbourne Sydney Auckland
Johannesburg and agencies throughout the world

www.watershipdown.net

1 3 5 7 9 10 8 6 4 2

Printed in China by Midas Printing Limited

THE RANDOM HOUSE GROUP Limited Reg. No. 954009

www.randomhouse.co.uk

ISBN 0 09 941105 9

This story represents scenes from the television
series, Watership Down, which is inspired by
Richard Adams' novel of the same name.

It was nearly Christmas and young Pipkin was very excited. 'We're going to have a huge feast and invite everyone!' he squeaked.

Hazel and Bigwig were not so happy. The food store was nearly empty.

'How can we make a feast of dried-up roots?' said Bigwig. 'Maybe we should cancel it.'

'We can't let the warren down!' said Hazel. 'We'll just have to raid the farm.'

It was snowing when Hazel and his friends set off.

'Be careful,' said Primrose, anxiously.

'Don't worry,' said Hazel. 'We'll be back soon. I promise.'

The rabbits followed Kehaar through some pine woods and into a field. There, they huddled under a wheatsheaf.

'Are we going the right way?' asked Hazel. 'We should have seen the farm lights by now.'

'I think so,' said Bigwig. 'But everything looks so different in the snow.'

'Well I'm not taking any chances,' said Hazel, firmly. 'Kehaar!' he called. 'Can you lead us back home?'

'Follow me,' squawked the gull. 'I lead. You follow.'

The rabbits followed Kehaar until they came to a river. It was partly frozen and black patches of water showed through the thin layer of ice.

'Is this a shortcut home, Kehaar? asked Hawkbit. 'This isn't *our* river.'

The gull shook his head. 'Must be a new river,' he said.

'Well, it's new to us,' said Hazel. 'We're lost!'

Suddenly Bigwig sat up. 'Ssh!' he hissed. 'There's a fox!'

The rabbits watched as a fox crept out of the reeds.

'Quick – cross the river!' urged Bigwig. 'Now!'

Bigwig waited as each rabbit slid across the ice, then he followed. Over his shoulder, he saw that the fox was on his trail. He went quickly but, in the middle of the river, the thin ice started to crack. With a cry, the big rabbit fell into the freezing water.

'Hang on, Bigwig, I'm coming,' said Hazel, crawling towards him.

'No! Get back,' said Bigwig.

The fox started to move towards Hazel. He was almost upon him when Kehaar swooped down from the sky.

The gull battered the fox with his wings and pecked at his nose. 'Leave my friends alone!' he screeched.

While Kehaar attacked the fox, Hazel pulled Bigwig out of the water and dragged him onto the bank.

'Let me lie down,' gasped Bigwig. 'Just need a minute to sleep…'

'Not now,' urged Hazel. 'You must keep moving.'

Bigwig staggered forwards. He was shivering with cold and covered in ice.

Slowly, the rabbits continued through the snow until they came to some tall iron gates.

'Follow me,' said Hazel, hopping through the bars. 'We can shelter under those trees.'

'I go look at stars,' said Kehaar. 'High above clouds. Stars show way home.'

After a short time, the rabbits heard the sound of bells.
They peeped out of the trees and saw a sleigh go by.

'Let's follow it,' said Hazel. 'We might find a warm place
where Bigwig can rest.'

The sleigh tracks led to a beautiful big house. The
rabbits crept up to a window and peeped inside.

'Have you ever seen so much food?' said Dandelion.
'Mmm, it smells so good!'

He was interrupted by someone coughing behind them.
It was a plump rabbit with a smiling face. 'Hello,' the
stranger said. 'I'm Buttercup. Who are you?'

'I'm Hazel,' said Hazel. 'And these are my friends.'

'You look cold,' said Buttercup. 'Every rabbit should be
in a warm burrow on Frith's Eve. Come with me.'

Buttercup led the rabbits across the lawn and into a maze.

As Hazel looked up at the tall hedges, he spotted Kehaar
flying high above them. 'Down here!' he shouted.

But the gull didn't hear and flew straight on. He circled
over the trees where he'd last seen his friends, but the

resting place was empty – all he could see was a fox.

'Ahh! Fox got friends!' he squawked and, wailing sadly, he flew back to Watership Down.

As Kehaar's cries faded away, Hawkbit sighed. 'Well, that's just great! How will we find our way home without him?'

In the centre of the maze, Buttercup stopped. 'Here we are,' she said. 'Home.'

Fiver looked up at the neat, square hedges. 'I don't know if I like this place,' he muttered. 'It's so unnatural.'

'I know,' said Hazel. 'But we must get Bigwig into a warm burrow – he's frozen!'

Inside, they settled Bigwig down in a soft corner, where he fell asleep at once.

'What brings you here?' asked Buttercup.

'We were out looking for food,' said Hazel. 'We got lost.'

Buttercup looked concerned. 'Come here,' she said, going across to a food store. 'Take all you need.'

When Kehaar arrived back at Watership Down, Pipkin ran to meet him. 'Where are Hazel and the others?' he asked.

The gull hung his head. 'Gone,' he said. 'Not coming back.'

'Gone where?' asked Pipkin.

'Just gone. No tracks. Just fox.' said Kehaar.

But Pipkin would not believe him. 'They're not gone,' he said. 'Hazel promised he'd come back – and Hazel keeps his promises.'

Suddenly Kehaar looked more cheerful. 'Yah, you right. I go back. Kehaar look again.'

At the maze warren, the rabbits had eaten well, and all the food was nearly finished.

'There's lots more outside,' said Buttercup. 'Will you come and help?'

'Of course,' said Hazel. He hopped across to where Fiver and Bigwig were sitting. 'We're going out, Fiver,' he said. 'I want you to stay with Bigwig.'

'Fiver's the one who needs watching,' laughed Bigwig. 'He's got the tingles about something.'

Hazel looked alarmed. 'What is it?' he asked.

'Maybe it's because we're so close to Man,' said Fiver. 'But there's danger nearby.'

'Don't worry,' said Hazel. 'We'll be extra careful.' And he followed Buttercup out of the burrow.

Underneath an old apple tree was a pile of carrots and cabbages. Hazel looked at the food suspiciously.

'It's all fresh,' said Buttercup. 'Man leaves it here every morning.'

Hazel backed away. 'Take us back to our friends,' he said. 'Now!'

Buttercup was surprised. 'We've only just got here,' she said. 'But if that's what you want…'

'We can't trust rabbits who take food from Man,' Hazel whispered to Hawkbit and Dandelion. 'We're better off lost than staying here – we must leave tonight.'

When the mansion rabbits were asleep, Hazel and his friends started to creep outside.

Then, all of a sudden, Buttercup appeared. 'Where do you think you're going?' she cried.

'Run!' Bigwig shouted. 'I'll fight her off!'

The frightened rabbits raced away and disappeared into the dark maze.

'We tried to help you, and now you attack us,' said Buttercup. 'Why?'

'You live alongside Man.' Bigwig replied. 'That makes you our enemy!'

Buttercup shook her head. 'You don't understand. Not all humans are alike. Here, Man is our friend and gives us food as a gift. Trust me.'

Inside the maze, the rabbits dashed along the twisting paths.

'There's no way out!' said Dandelion, as they came to a dead end.

Hazel led his friends back the way they'd come. But around the next corner they bumped into the fox.

'Run!' said Hazel, turning and racing down another path.

High above, Kehaar had returned and was looking at the ground below. He saw the fox chasing the rabbits through the maze.

'Hazel! I save you from fox,' screeched the gull. 'Go where I say!'

Kehaar led the rabbits back into the centre of the maze, where a group of humans were singing songs around a Christmas tree.

'What do we do now?' gasped Hawkbit. 'How can we get back to the warren?'

'Run through their legs!' urged Hazel.

As the rabbits dodged in and out of the humans' legs, the fox came charging round the corner. When he saw the humans, he skidded to a halt, and then turned back into the shadows.

'Hah!' said Kehaar. 'Man scare fox plenty!'

The rabbits tumbled into Buttercup's burrow, where Bigwig
was very pleased to see them. 'That looked close.' he said.
'But you're safe here.'

Hazel looked shocked. 'What! With Man just outside?'

'We were wrong,' said Bigwig. 'These humans won't hurt
us – apparently they like us!'

'It was the fox I sensed,' said Fiver. 'That was the danger,
not the humans.'

Buttercup smiled. 'Just as Man offers us his food and
friendship, I offer you ours. Let's take a feast back to
Watership Down!'

Pipkin couldn't believe his eyes when he saw
the rabbits coming up the hill with carrots
and cabbages, turnips and radishes.

'I knew you'd come back!' he said.

'Now we can have the best feast ever!'
laughed Hazel, as they laid out the food.
'Thanks to all our new friends.'

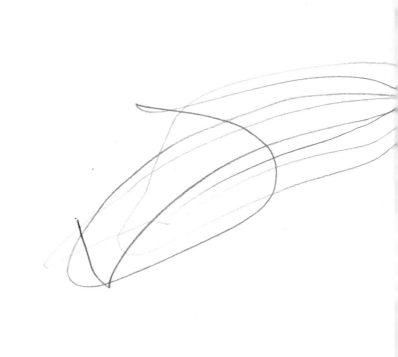